OTHER TIMES AND PLACES

SEVEN TALES OF THE FANTASTIC

JOE MAHONEY

DONOVAN STREET PRESS

Donovan Street Press Inc.

Edited by Dr. Robert Runté.

Issued in print and electronic formats.

Library and Archives Canada Cataloguing in Publication

Title: Other times and places / Joe Mahoney.

Other titles: Short stories.

Names: Mahoney, Joe, 1965- author.

Description: Short stories. | Includes index.

Identifiers: Canadiana (print) 20190236469 | Canadiana (ebook) 20190236477 | ISBN 9780359868520

(softcover) | ISBN 9780359841820 (ebook)

Classification: LCC PS8626 .A417415 2020 | DDC C813/.6—dc23

❀ Created with Vellum

For Ryley
who told me not to settle

PUBLICATION HISTORY

"Moonstone" originally appeared in *The Sword Review* and was reprinted in the anthology *Distant Passages: The Best from Double-Edged Publishing*, 2005, Bill Snodgrass, ed. Cordova, Tennessee: Double-Edged Publishing, 2006.

"The Wizard's Castle" originally appeared as "A Fresh Pair of Eyes" in *Horizons SF* 20, no. 2 (1999). [University of British Columbia's Science Fiction Society, Ryan Hawe, ed]. Subsequently produced as audio play, "The Wizard's Castle" for *KidzAir*, Air Canada, 2005.

"Of Platypuses and Things", originally appeared in *Planet Relish*, no. 22. [Mark Rapacioli, ed.]

"The Pitch" appears here for the first time.

"Fizz" originally appeared in *Polar Borealis,* no. 3 (Nov/Dec 2016). [R. Graeme Cameron, ed.]

"The Scapegoat" originally appeared in *Challenging Destiny* 9, April 2000. David M. Switzer & Robert P. Switzer, eds.

"John's Worst Enemy" originally appeared in *SDO Fantasy* [Sintrigue Dot Org] and reprinted in *The Best of SDO*, Mark Anthony Brennan & David Bowlin, eds. Subsequently translated into Greek and published in *Ennea* no. 9 [Angelos Mastorakis, ed.]

"The Screw-up" originally appeared in *Our Times: Canada's Independent Labour Magazine, 2000.*

FOREWORD

Covering nearly twenty years, this collection of Joe Mahoney's short fiction (cleverly entitled *Other Times and Places* in a nod to his debut novel *A Time and a Place*) provides a good overview of Joe Mahoney's career leading up to that novel. Presumably you found this collection having read *A Time and A Place*, and googled to see what else Joe's written. Well, this is the rest of his fiction, so far. Those unfamiliar with Joe's writing can be assured of the collection's quality by the implied endorsement of their previous selection and publication by several magazine and anthology editors. Indeed, the observant reader will note that three of the seven stories that appear here were doubly endorsed by being reprinted in a 'best of' collection, translated into another language, or adapted for audio. To complete the collection—and to force fans to buy the collection even if they've already read all the others—Joe has generously included one never-before-seen story.

The collection is nicely balanced between science fiction and fantasy, humorous and serious, sweet and sinister. What I like most about Joe's stories is that they all have something to say. Just as *A Time and a Place* has a lot more going on below the surface than the frantic action might at first suggest, the narratives in these stories carry one along through social satire or theological consideration or provide a quick glimpse at the behind the scenes machinations at CBC radio. (By the way if you *haven't* read *A Time and A Place* yet, stop what you're doing and go get a copy. It's a ridiculously riveting read.)

Of course, the chief purpose of acquiring this collection is so one can pretend to have discovered Joe's fiction two decades ago and to have been following his career this whole time. "It was obvious he had a great novel in him," you could say, and claim you had had the foresight to start collecting his stories before his other fans had even heard of him. Feel free to proclaim, "You can't really appreciate *A Time and a Place* without understanding where it fits within the context of the whole of Joe's canon," safe in the knowledge that there is no way the listener is going to be able to track down a copy of, say, *Challenging Destiny 9* to check if that's true.

It's possible some of you are actually here for the stories themselves. Short fiction is enjoying a bit of a renaissance these days, as evidenced by the many more print and online magazines out there, and short SF&F makes the best reading for those commuting or otherwise needing a bit of a break in their day. And fans of *A Time and a Place* obviously need something to read while awaiting Joe's next novel.

Well then, carry on!

Robert Runté
  September, 2019

1

MOONSTONE

The shopkeeper consulted his parchment, then counted on his fingertips. "That will be eight guild, if you please."

Tanner Kyle reached for his pouch and found nothing. His heart gave a lurch. He felt for the oilskin packet concealed in an inside pocket and fingered the telltale lump just long enough to confirm its presence there. He relaxed, just a bit. Smart to have separated the amulet from the coin. Still, the theft of the pouch did promise to make life difficult.

"We've been robbed," he announced.

Keele Wren glanced up from the scroll he was perusing. "Ah," he said. "The irony."

Tanner concluded that 'irony' must be

another word for amulet. "Safe," he said. "We only lost the coin."

Keele arched an eyebrow.

"I don't suppose you—never mind." Tanner knew very well that Keele's oath prevented him from carrying coin of any kind. "I don't understand how the rascal even got close to me. You did have wards in place, didn't you? Against theft, loss, that sort of thing?"

Keele eyed the sword sheathed at Tanner's side. "We needed wards?"

Tanner ripped the severed drawstring from his belt and flung it on the floor. "My blade will serve us well enough when we find the scoundrel who robbed us. I'll use it to skin and gut him if he has any meat on his bones. He'll be all we have to eat in Fanarion now that we can't afford food."

The shopkeeper grimaced. "Surely it won't come to that. I'd be quite happy to barter."

Tanner eyed the shopkeeper's squat body, wiry black hair, and flat, misshapen nose. Any fool could see that the blood of a gnome coursed through this one. Tanner's father had often regaled him with stories about gnomes.

Stories full of greed, and cunning. "What do they call you?" he asked.

"Darvin, son of Neek."

"What did you have in mind, Neekson?"

Neekson's eyes settled on Tanner's sword, a slender affair that Tanner kept polished and well oiled.

"I think not," Tanner said.

"Of course not."

Tanner turned to Keele. "Anything you could stand to part with?"

"A compendium of indigenous waterfowl," Keele suggested.

"Birds," Neekson translated, tapping his fingers on the lid of a barrel. "That won't do, I'm afraid."

Keele returned his attention to the scroll.

The staccato of Neekson's fingernails on the barrel grated on Tanner's nerves. He considered hastening matters, unsheathing his blade and stealing the goods they needed. But that would only bring the city guard down upon him, and the last thing he needed was more people chasing him.

He smiled toothily. "I could let you have some furs."

"Plenty of furs left over from last winter."

Tanner's grin faded as he considered his options. Perhaps, between his bow and Keele's arts, they would be able to make do in Fanarion without supplies. But no, that would be foolhardy. The same qualities that made Fanarion such an ideal hiding place—a scarcity of game and water, a reputation for transforming stolid, capable men into barking lunatics—made it a destination not to be taken lightly. You had to be half a fool to venture into Fanarion at all, let alone without supplies.

Tanner took the oilskin packet from inside his coat, unwrapped it, and set the contents on the barrel in front of Neekson. He felt Keele's eyes upon him as he did so.

Neekson sucked in his breath at what he saw.

"You know what this is," Tanner said. "What it's worth."

"Of course," Neekson said. "It's my business to know. But it's of no use to me."

"Why not?"

"I don't deal in such things."

"You don't deal in gems?"

"I don't deal in objects of darkness forged in secret by warped craftsmen for the sole purpose of robbing men and women of just about everything they have. Including themselves. If I were you I would cast this thing aside, somewhere no one will find it."

"It doesn't frighten me the way it seems to frighten some."

"It ought to." Neekson studied Tanner. "Anyway, you'll be wanting more than a few quarrels and blankets for the likes of this. I don't keep that kind of coin on hand."

"You could get it."

"No," Neekson said, "I could not."

Tanner put the amulet away. "You're right, I want more than a few blankets, a lot more. Keep my goods together, gnome. I'll be back with the coin."

Neekson closed his eyes. "There's no such thing as gnomes," he said, through clenched teeth.

A gnome who didn't believe in gnomes? Tanner could not help but chuckle on his way out.

A worn sign depicting a single gauntlet swayed in the breeze outside the

Heroes Welcome. At the door, a sinewy woman with two short swords slung low at her hips looked Tanner over but said nothing. The common room was well populated despite the early hour. Tanner walked slowly between thick oak tables stretching from one end of the room to the other, admiring a variety of stuffed animal heads affixed to the walls, several species of which he didn't recognise.

He chose a table beneath the mildewed tusk of one such enormous beast.

"Innkeeper," he called out. "Mead. Hot."

He yanked off a boot and shook out one of two copper pieces he kept hidden for just such a predicament as this. He struggled to get the boot back on, then straightened up to find a steaming hot mug of mead on the table before him.

The innkeeper, a grizzled sort, lingered nearby clearing a table.

"Place like this must see no small spot of trouble," Tanner said.

"Aye, that it does."

"Just the one keeping your peace?" Tanner jerked a thumb toward the woman lurking in the entrance. Though easily half again

Tanner's age, she appeared fit and well muscled.

"Don't let Leese fool you," the innkeeper said. "Tougher than old leather, that one."

Tanner wasn't fooled. He had plenty of respect for the likes of Leese, having fought beside several just like her. "Could you use another?"

"Nope."

"Just for the day?"

"Nope."

Tanner grunted his dissatisfaction and watched as Keele strode into the common room. Keele had to bend slightly to avoid hitting his head on top of the doorframe.

Leese looked the other way as Keele entered. Keele's vocation was unmistakable, with his drooping moustaches, black robes, and especially the owl ring adorning the third finger of his left hand. Only a fool messed with a man like Keele. If such a fool were lucky and didn't die a grisly death right away, he might wake up several nights in a row screaming, covered from head to toe in large, black spiders. Hairy ones, with long legs. Tanner shuddered at the memory—never again would he criticise Keele's cooking.

Neekson trailed Keele into the inn, struggling to keep up. Leese had no qualms about stopping him before he got very far.

"Your kind isn't welcome here," Leese said, her voice carrying easily to Tanner's side of the room. "As you well know."

Keele pushed his billowing cloak aside and sat down opposite Tanner.

"What's the gnome doing in here?"Tanner asked him.

Keele shrugged. "Perhaps he found your coin."

Tanner whirled on the innkeeper. "Let him in."

"And why would you be wanting the likes of that in here?"

"Just let him in."

The innkeeper called to Leese, "Let him pass. See that he doesn't hurt anyone."

Several patrons guffawed at the innkeeper's wit. Tanner chuckled himself.

Leese slapped Neekson on the backside with the flat of her blade. Neekson scurried away to avoid being hit again and reached Tanner's table out of breath.

"You can have the goods you asked for,"

he told Tanner, glancing nervously over his shoulder.

"That's very generous."

"In exchange for—"

"What?"

Neekson faced Keele. "I want you to make me strong."

He was either very brave or an ignorant fool. Many in Keele's Order would have turned him into a steaming pile of manure just for asking. Tanner edged back from the table just in case; he didn't want shit on his good fur cloak.

Keele inspected his one-inch long fingernails. "Why?"

Neekson stole a glance at Leese, then returned his gaze to Keele. He didn't say anything. He didn't need to.

Tanner had a jibe on the tip of his tongue but Keele silenced him with a look. Tanner felt a thrill of fear. Neekson had aroused Keele's interest—whether for good or ill remained to be seen.

The innkeeper approached. "I let you in, now do you spit on my hospitality?"

"I beg your pardon," Neekson said. "I'll have, ah. . ."

"An ale," Tanner said. "Make that two."

Keele's accent sometimes got the better of him, and he said something now that not even Tanner could understand. Clearly afraid to ask Keele to repeat himself, the innkeeper nodded and backed away.

"My father used to say that strength without honour is like a wolf with no teeth," Tanner said. "Strong today, food for the buzzards tomorrow."

"I have honour. My word is important to me."

Tanner chuckled. "Then you're stronger than me already."

"You don't understand—"

"I understand perfectly," Tanner interrupted. "You want to be strong. Keele makes you strong, you give us the goods we need. What do you say, Keele? The sooner we get out of here the better."

"You ask a lot of me," Keele said.

Neekson's chin rose. Amber eyes locked onto brown. Neekson held Keele's eyes for a good four seconds before jerking his head away.

Keele's moustache twitched. He produced a blank parchment from within his cloak and a bottle of black ink and a quill from another pocket. He began inscribing elegantly formed symbols on the parchment.

The innkeeper arrived and plunked three drinks down in front of them. Neekson paid for all three of them. Tanner took a belt of ale and tried to guess what all the symbols on Keele's parchment meant. Across from him, Neekson fidgeted restlessly.

Keele finished and handed the parchment to Neekson. "I require one of everything on the list. Except for the horn of rhinoceros."

Neekson looked up.

"I need two of them."

Neekson opened his mouth, then closed it.

"Can you do it?" Tanner asked.

"I don't know. I'll try. I have certain... contacts. I'll do what I can."

"You will get it all," Keele said. "By twilight. Or you will never be strong."

Neekson nodded and stuffed the list inside his cloak. On his way out, Leese mussed his hair and pinched his bottom.

Tanner placed his mug on the table. "Think making him strong will do him any good?"

Keele wasn't listening. He spat on the table, then glared in the direction of the innkeeper. "I did not ask for cow's milk," he said.

Tanner grimaced and wondered how the innkeeper felt about spiders.

———

Twilight found Tanner sitting beneath the same gargantuan tusk staring sourly into the mug of ale he had just purchased with his last copper. It irked him that after only two swigs precious little ale remained in the mug. That wasn't all that was bothering him. The stable master had just informed him that he owed two guild for the lodging of his horses—two guild more than he possessed. Two guards had lurked menacingly behind the stable master as he spoke.

It would not do to lose the horses. If Neekson ever showed up—and Tanner was growing skeptical on this count—he could find himself with plenty of goods but no animals to carry them. If that happened, he might have no choice but to steal the animals back. He remembered the two stable guards, and almost laughed aloud. He risked all of a stubbed toe confronting the likes of them.

Problem was, Keele would not approve. He had adamantly refused to have anything to do with the theft of the amulet.

"I am a scholar, not a thief," he had stated firmly when Tanner informed him of his plan.

"Is it the oath you took?" Tanner asked him. Oaths were something he could understand, having sworn several himself, none of which he could remember in any detail.

"It has nothing to do with my oath."

Tanner was not offended. Keele was a different sort of man, his code was not Tanner's code, that of the surly miners with whom Tanner and his father had lived in near poverty. Rough-hewn men carving coal out of the Blue Shank Mountains. Or those with whom they had later dwelt and whom Tanner admired most, men of dark humour and lightning fast blades, who took what they wanted when they wanted. Gold from dead men's teeth, land from arrogant lords, gems off the slender white necks of vain young noblewomen.

Tanner's plan had revolved around one

such creature basking in the moonlight on a remote part of her family's estate—just as a certain gentleman in Lycatos had said she would be. A simple throat lock made a fool of her inattentive guardian, and Damaris Fen—that was what the fellow in Lycatos had called her, along with other, less flattering names—did not stir as Tanner stole upon her.

Clutching his dagger in one hand, Tanner took hold of the amulet with the other. A flush of warmth spread from the top of his head to the tips of his toes. Attributing the sensation to nerves, he dismissed it, and lifted the amulet from Damaris' bosom. It felt cool in his palm. He marveled at the intricacy of the engravings on its rim, at the beauty of the crystalline stone set within. A diamond, if Tanner's loose-lipped acquaintance could be believed—and though half in his cups, the fellow had been right about everything else.

A sharp tug freed the chain from Damaris' neck. She awoke and felt where the amulet had been. When she did not find it, and spied Tanner crouching beside her, she sat up abruptly. She wrapped her arms around her shoulders and sat utterly still, looking at him.

Tanner was transfixed by the look of her.

Not because she was the beauty the unhappy fellow in Lycatos had professed her to be—there was a child-like quality to her features that did not appeal to Tanner—it was that he had never seen a woman look half so well scrubbed before.

When Damaris opened her mouth to speak Tanner shushed her by placing a finger to his lips. He feared that her retainers might be lingering near the edge of the woods, not so far away.

She spoke anyway, her voice tremulous. "It was a gift—"

Tanner clapped a hand across her mouth and clutched her to him. "Not a word," he whispered, brandishing his dagger before a pair of widening eyes.

Damaris' scent, like that of a freshly bitten peach, enveloped Tanner, made him acutely aware that it was the flesh of a woman beneath his callused hands. He felt her tremble beneath his embrace. She probably thought that he intended to claim another, more ignoble prize.

Tanner released her. "Quiet," he commanded, as her weeping became audible.

The request was futile.

The fear of being discovered overtook Tanner and he fled back through the woods with his prize. Any misgivings he might have felt for having terrorized Damaris he dismissed as foolishness. Not a single drop of blood had been shed, and such an amulet, worth more than Tanner might honestly earn in his lifetime, was surely but a bauble to the likes of her.

On the road to Wyrth, Keele sat astride his grey and examined the amulet for no more than two seconds before handing it back to Tanner.

"Moonstone," Keele said. "Not diamond."

"Moonstone? Never heard of it."

"A particularly nasty indulgence of the rich."

"What do you mean?"

"She wore it in the glen, you say. Under the light of a full moon."

"As was her habit, I'm told."

"That does not strike you as peculiar?"

Tanner shrugged. "She's rich. Rich people do all sorts of strange things."

Keele regarded Tanner for several long seconds. Finally he said, "Do not wear it against your skin, or handle it any more than necessary, especially in moonlight. Try not to look at it. As soon as you can, get rid of it."

"Why? What's wrong with it?"

Keele twisted in his saddle and squinted down the road behind them. "She will come for it."

Tanner snorted. That much he knew already. Mere bauble or not, the House of Fen would soon be after him. The rich did not like to be trifled with. Brimming with wrath and righteous indignation, they would hang Tanner from the highest tree for his effrontery, if they could find him. They might find him in Wyrth, if they tried hard enough.

They would not find him in Fanarion.

Leese's throaty voice jarred Tanner back to the present. "I'll throw you out by the scruff of the neck if I have to."

Tanner looked up to see Leese looming over Neekson, who struggled under the weight of a large sack. Neekson said something that Tanner couldn't quite make out.

A beefy man clad in the burnished leather of the city guard snatched the sack away from Neekson and emptied its contents onto the floor. He snapped up one of the objects and held it aloft. "He brings wares to sell to the kitchen. A bat! He would have us eat this filthy vermin."

"It's not for sale." Neekson made a grab for the bat, but the guard held it just out of reach.

Keele emerged from his room at the top of the stairs.

Tanner scrambled to his feet—he had to do something before Keele turned the guard into a toad, or worse. By the time he made it to the entrance, though, Keele was already there, and Neekson was on his hands and knees chasing around a duck. Neekson's tormentor was nowhere to be seen.

"You'll turn the entire inn against us!" Tanner whispered to Keele.

Keele looked over Tanner's shoulder. Tanner spun to see Leese ushering the guard outside. The duck had come from Neekson's sack, he realised.

Keele's moustache twitched. "Come with me," he said. "You too, Neekson."

Keele led them to the room he shared with Tanner. Neekson cast nervous glances behind them the entire way. In the room, a small array of glass tubes, bottles and jars littered a rickety table in the corner. Much of the apparatus was coated with a greenish residue. The room itself smelled of burnt incense. Keele placed the sack under the table and passed Neekson a small vial containing a yellowish solution.

Tanner had drunk Keele's concoctions before. He made a face but held his tongue. He didn't want to discourage Neekson from drinking the solution. Neekson lifted the vial to his mouth and drank the fluid down without a second's hesitation. He coughed and twisted his face in a grimace but seemed otherwise unaffected.

"I don't feel any different," he said. "You haven't even used the goods I spent all day collecting."

"They will be put to good use. In a stew I am preparing."

Neekson stared at the empty vial in his hand. "You've taken me for a fool."

"Perhaps," Keele said. "Just the same, you will be strong tomorrow."

"But I'm still small."

"On the outside. You will be strong on the inside."

Tanner agreed with Neekson that he didn't

look any different, but he knew better than to underestimate Keele Wren.

"Uh oh." Neekson steadied himself on the table.

Tanner had been waiting for this. When Neekson's legs buckled, Tanner was there to catch him.

Beads of moisture appeared on Neekson's forehead. "You've killed me!"

"You will run a high fever tonight," Keele said. "You will sleep through most of it, and dream of the past, the present, and the future. When you wake up, you will be strong."

Neekson tried to say something but it came out as gibberish. Tanner placed him on Keele's pallet, where he lay sweating and gasping for air.

"He will be fine," Keele assured Tanner.

"What about you?" The night would hold more challenges for Keele, Tanner suspected, than it would for Neekson.

"I will be fine too."

Tanner nodded and left.

Laughter and the stench of stale ale greeted Tanner at the bottom of the stairs, too much of each. Slipping out back of the Heroes Welcome for some fresh air and quiet, he succumbed to the temptation to inspect his prize. He removed the oilskin from its hiding place, carefully uncovered the amulet, and admired it in the day's fading light.

Despite his caution, the amulet chanced to brush Tanner's skin. A shock of pleasure swept over him, utterly unlike anything he had ever experienced before. It left him breathless, made him yearn to touch the amulet again, but he resisted, though it took all his will to do so.

With great care, he put the amulet away. He thought about asking Keele more about it, but decided not to. Keele would tell him to get rid of it, and this Tanner would not do. Not until he could sell it for the kind of coin other men spent entire lives pining for. Embittered men, health and spirits broken. Men doomed to shallow graves.

Smarter, bolder than his father, Tanner would neither live nor die like him.

I n the morning, Keele sat cross-legged on his pallet, his eyes closed, a thin blue vein pulsing high in his forehead. From time to time he placed a hand on the floor to steady himself.

Neekson sat breaking his fast at the table. Tanner joined him.

"I feel better than ever," Neekson said, between heaping mouthfuls of stew. "Maybe that potion did something after all."

Keele opened one bloodshot eye.

"I dreamt, too, just as you said I would. There were enemies all about me. I cut men down with a terrible sword, cut them down by the score, and I was stronger than I ever imagined possible, and finally I grew tired and I wanted to lie down but I couldn't, my enemies kept on coming. I couldn't see the end of them." Neekson placed his spoon down on the table. "What does it mean, a dream like that?"

"Something you ate," Tanner said.

The others looked at him.

"I have dreams like that all the time," he explained.

Keele said, "There is a woman in Lycatos who knows a thing or two about dreams. Perhaps you should ask her."

Neekson nodded. "I might just do that."

After consuming a dish of Keele's

succulent stew himself, Tanner led Neekson to the smithy next door to determine just how effective Keele's labours had been. They walked in on the blacksmith holding a horseshoe in place with a pair of iron tongs. Ropy muscles bulged beneath the blacksmith's filthy tunic as he pounded on the glowing object.

"I'm busy," he told Tanner. "Come back later, tomorrow maybe. Next week."

"We're not looking to hire you."

"What then?"

Tanner nodded toward the anvil the blacksmith was using. "We want to borrow that."

"What the devil for?"

"To see if I can lift it," Neekson said.

The blacksmith placed the freshly formed horseshoe in a bucket of icy water. The water hissed and frothed as the horseshoe cooled. "I told you, I'm busy. Take your drunken nonsense someplace else."

Before the blacksmith could stop him, Neekson strode toward the anvil and gripped it with both hands. When he straightened up, the anvil rose with him.

Tanner whistled. "Set it down now,

carefully," he said. "Bend your knees, not your back."

Neekson did as Tanner instructed.

"What devilry is this?" The blacksmith wiped sweat from his brow with the back of his hand. "I can't move that anvil without a team of oxen."

Tanner had witnessed Keele accomplish several mind-boggling feats in the time that he'd known him, yet even he was impressed.

Neekson stood stock still, staring at his hands. His mien had darkened. "Let them mock me now."

"Give me the goods you promised me," Tanner said, "or I'll do more than mock you."

"You'll have your goods," Neekson said. "Just—I need time to get them together."

Tanner recalled his father's profound distrust of gnomes. But Neekson would have Keele to contend with if he tried anything foolish. Either way, Tanner would get his goods. "Be quick about it," he said. "We're in a hurry."

S our red beans and water the colour of urine constituted board at the Heroes Welcome. Tanner toyed with the beans, then forced himself to eat every last one. He meant to be in Fanarion by late afternoon, and a man wanted a full belly before setting foot in a place like that.

The innkeeper placed a mug on the table. Startled, Tanner stuck his nose over the brim. It smelled like wine. Tanner hadn't drunk wine—real wine—in over a year.

The innkeeper sat down beside him. He had dark circles under his eyes that had not been there the day before. "Seems I've offended your friend," he said. "Had dealings with his kind before, you know. Snakes there were, dozens of them. Lucky to get out of there alive. Be the same tonight, won't it?"

Tanner bid the innkeeper lean closer. "You served him cow's milk, a terrible mistake. Keele considers cows holy, or mystical, or some damned thing."

The innkeeper rubbed his temple with a knuckle, hard. "Don't want to have to go through another night like that one."

Tanner thought about the coin he owed

the stable master. "You could make it up to him."

The innkeeper sighed. "I was afraid you'd say something like that. How much do you want?"

The idea that Tanner had any real influence over Keele was absurd, but the innkeeper had no way of knowing that. Tanner fiddled with his mug. Wine slopped over the brim and onto the table.

The innkeeper peered at him, waiting.

"Two guild," Tanner said. There was no way around it, not if he wanted his horses back.

The innkeeper refused to look Tanner in the eye. He gave Tanner the coin and left. Afterward, Tanner sampled the wine and made a face. It was real wine all right, but only just. He took another slug of the stuff just the same.

Catching a glimpse of Neekson coming through the entrance Tanner spat the wine out all over the table. Clad in complete battle regalia, everything Neekson wore was too large by half. Chain mail drooped below his knees. His helm refused to stay put over his eyes. Tanner wondered at the gnome's ability to walk in the outrageous outfit, but walk he could, for he strode right up and pressed a short sword firmly against Leese's belly.

The door warden's lips curled in disbelief at the sight of Neekson's costume. She pushed Neekson's sword aside with a finger. "What in the Seven Levels of Hell are you?"

"I want in. Let me in."

Leese sighed. "You're not welcome here, gnome."

All the life seemed to go out of Neekson. He lowered both sword and gaze. Then, issuing a loud cry, he struck, neither quickly nor assuredly, yet the force of the blow was enough to tear Leese's hastily drawn weapon from her grasp and send it clattering to the floor.

"Sorcery," Leese observed, retrieving her weapon. Rising and twisting all in one motion, she struck Neekson full on the chest, sending him aloft in a shower of sparks. Neekson came crashing to the floor half a span from where he had been standing.

Neekson rose to his feet, scowling. The expression did not make him any prettier. A large dent was visible in his armour, yet he appeared unharmed.

Leese offered up a series of short, probing jabs. It soon became painfully obvious that Neekson did not know the first thing about wielding a sword. He countered Leese's advances gamely enough, but his own clumsy forays Leese swept aside with about as much effort as a cat batting aside an errant whisker.

The time came to end the charade. Leese stepped in deftly and slapped Neekson on the side of the head with the flat of her blade. Neekson's eyes rolled back in his head and he crumpled to the floor. Leese lugged him unceremoniously out of the Heroes Welcome by the straps of his breastplate and was back inside the Heroes Welcome seconds later as if nothing at all untoward had happened.

Tanner suspected that for a woman like Leese, in a place like the Heroes Welcome, nothing had.

He found Neekson sitting forlornly on the front steps of the Heroes Welcome with his helm off, a small, purplish bruise marring his left temple. Kneeling, Tanner made to examine the bruise but Neekson shied away.

"Neekson," Tanner said. "Look at me."

Neekson lifted his chin.

Leese had landed at least one blow that

would have cracked an ordinary man's ribs, yet Tanner could find no evidence of it. After a brief but thorough inspection, he said, "You'll live. Thanks to Keele's arts, I expect."

Neekson muttered something under his breath.

"What did you say?"

"I said that's something, at least."

"Figured to best her easily, did you? Suppose you thought it would be enough to be strong." Tanner sat down at Neekson's side. "What you need to do is find yourself a master. Throw yourself at his mercy. Beg him to teach you everything he knows. Train morning, noon and night for seven years. Then find Leese again."

Neekson looked at him as if he were mad. "Seven years?"

"In your case, maybe eight."

A horse approached at a gallop; Keele's grey, wild-eyed and frothing at the bit. Keele reined up in front of the two men, looking little better than he had that morning. A woman sat behind him, her arms wrapped tightly about his waist, her head resting between his shoulder blades.

The grey pranced sideways. With a shock

that brought him to his feet, Tanner recognised the woman as Damaris Fen. She didn't look quite so freshly scrubbed anymore. Burrs dotted her hair. Streaks of mud and blood discoloured her cheeks and fingernails. Tanner tried to wrap his head around her presence on the back of Keele's grey, and couldn't, quite.

Keele regarded Tanner from atop the grey. "Is it her?"

Tanner felt a sinking in his gut, a feeling he got whenever his luck was about to change, and not for the better. "Yes, but—"

"Good," Keele said, dismounting.

"What are you doing with her?"

"Found her. Off the King's Road, alone."

"Alone? You're sure about that?"

Keele did not deign to answer.

"You mean no one's after us?"

"No one except her."

"I don't understand. What about her family? What's the matter with her, anyway?"

"It's the moonstone," Keele said.

Neekson's head jerked up like a small rodent sensing danger.

"What about the moonstone?" Tanner

asked, although he did not really want to know.

"It's killing her," Keele said, easing Damaris down off the grey.

T he whites of Damaris' eyes flickered beneath half-closed eyelids. Beads of spittle pooled at the corners of her mouth. But for Keele's grasp, she might have fallen.

"How could it be killing her?" Tanner asked. "She's not even wearing it."

Keele eased Damaris gently onto the steps of the Heroes Welcome. "You took the moonstone from her. In turn, the moonstone took her mind. It's not unheard of."

Damaris had suffered more than just injury to her mind. Countless brambles and thorns had torn the clothes from her back, flayed the skin from her face and body. Tanner watched as Keele applied salve to an ugly laceration on her face. "You went looking for her," he accused him. "You knew she would be out there."

"I am not a seer," Keele said. "I did not know for certain."

Why Keele would have gone out of his way to find Damaris Fen Tanner could not imagine. Keele's Order was not exactly known for their good works. Damaris was a Fen, of course, of the House of Fen, and a man stood to benefit greatly by aiding the likes of them, but Tanner did not think that was it. The Keele he knew served no man.

His voice pitched slightly higher than usual, he asked, "What if someone followed you? What then?"

Keele ignored him, and Tanner forced himself to let it go. In the end, Keele's act had done more good than harm. Now it was obvious that the House of Fen didn't know about the theft. Damaris had simply wandered off, into the woods, her mind addled by the abrupt loss of the moonstone. Her guardian, having failed to protect her, had almost certainly not alerted his superiors. If the House of Fen wasn't after Tanner, then it wasn't necessary to risk Fanarion. Tanner was free to travel inland, to Marjan maybe, or Wurzipal. Sell the amulet. Live like a king.

Neekson appeared at his side, his eyes fixed on Damaris. Tanner had almost forgotten about him.

"Give it back to her," Neekson said.

Tanner could hardly believe his ears. "Give it back?"

"Look at her. As it is she'll never be the same, if she lives. Do you understand that? Do you care?" Neekson's fists were white balls at his sides. "Or are you too busy figuring out how much silver and gold you're going to squeeze out of the thing that's killing her?"

Tanner flinched. "It wasn't my fault. I didn't know about the moonstone. I thought it was diamond—"

"You know now." Neekson's short sword hissed from its scabbard. "Give it back to her."

Tanner stepped back in alarm, fearing Neekson's lack of control with the weapon.

"Now." Neekson leveled the sword at Tanner's chest.

"And what good would that do?"

"Save her life, if we can wean her off it properly. If we're lucky. If she hasn't been wearing it too long. And that's not all. We need to make sure you don't sell it to anyone else." The point of Neekson's blade descended slowly, coming to rest lightly on

Tanner's chest. "We need to make sure that no one else suffers."

Tanner flicked his eyes from the sword to Neekson back to the sword again. His own sword exploded from its scabbard, searing a blistering path through the air that ripped Neekson's weapon from his hands and sent it careening away. A boot to the chest doubled Neekson over. Neekson collapsed to the ground gasping for breath, his knees drawn up close to his chest.

"Let me tell you a little something about suffering." Tanner's blade drew a slender, menacing shadow across Neekson's face. "About boys digging for coal with their bare hands. About black-lunged fathers boiling grass for their families to eat. Men and boys coughing up blood. Suffering. Dying. I've done my share of suffering, Neekson. I'll do no more of it."

"You'll make others suffer instead," Neekson wheezed, through lips drawn taut with pain. "Is that it?"

Tanner tightened his grip on his blade, tempted to end Neekson's suffering right then and there. Neekson's unnatural strength had clearly waned; a quick thrust to the neck should make him dead enough to satisfy most gods. He stared into Neekson's amber eyes, struggling to muster some strength of his own. The strength to kill a man over a cutting remark. To let a girl die over want of a few coin.

But that kind of strength Tanner did not possess. Would never possess. And so it was that he found himself handing the oilskin packet over to Keele, who, with clever fingers, mended the broken chain and slipped the amulet around Damaris' neck. Damaris opened her eyes, took in her surroundings. Keele's moustache twitched. It occurred to Tanner that he didn't know Keele quite as well as he thought he did.

Perhaps even less than he knew himself.

2

THE WIZARD'S CASTLE

The boy caught sight of what he had come to see half way up the mountain.

He gasped at the wonder of it all.

He saw among other things turrets and spires and slim, cylindrical towers, and when he got closer there was a drawbridge spanning a moat of an enchanting silvery liquid, and finally, a modest faerie mist clothing grey stone walls near where they met the earth. The wizard's castle was everything his imagination had said it would be.

When he stepped upon the drawbridge, though, he saw that the moat beneath him contained only water. Considering it had appeared infinitely more magical only moments before—perhaps the reflection of the sun had fooled him—he was slightly disappointed. Even so, he could not help but wonder what peculiar manner of creature lay in wait beneath the water's silvery sheen. Aside from sea serpents and sharks he could think of no names, but his mind drew terrible pictures, and he was careful to stay well to the centre of the drawbridge as he daringly traversed its length.

The boy paused at the far end of the drawbridge, dwarfed there by the enormous wooden door. He lifted his hand to knock but found that he could not. Instead, butterflies invaded his stomach and his mind whirled with fears. What if he had come all this way for nothing? Suppose the wizard did not receive visitors after all? Would he send the boy away? Or worse, in a fit of pique at having been disturbed, might the wizard wave his hands in the air and utter angry words that would transform his unwelcome visitor into a toad or a goblin?

Such a fate seemed entirely possible to the boy now that he had thought of it. Unnerved, he turned to flee, and he would have done so except that just then, accompanied by the sound of grinding gears and rattling chains, the huge wooden door slowly began to creak open, and the chance to flee was past.

A shock of unruly white hair surrounded a cherubic cheeked face. Eyes the reflection of a winter sky focused on the boy as the entire combination poked out from behind the door. A frown and a "breathe, boy, it doesn't do to hold one's breath," acknowledged the petrified lad. "Come for a visit, have you?"

The boy could only nod.

"Well, come in, come in. Have you a name? Perhaps when you find your tongue you can tell me what it is. Myself, I am the caretaker of this keep, and as such I must ask you to wipe your feet, please, this isn't a hovel, you know, it is a castle, and we must abide by certain rules. Rules are unfortunate, restricting things, but they do possess a certain merit, they keep the floors clean you'll notice, and if that is not a sufficient reason to abide by rules then I am unaware of what is," and accompanied by a great deal more rambling of a similar nature the boy was led inside.

Enormous tapestries lined walls of corridors guarded by uninhabited suits of shining armour. The footsteps of the caretaker and the boy could have been those of giants, rattling back and forth between the distant walls the way they did.

The boy began to relax as the words of the old man encircled and reassured him. It was good of him to come, very few did these days, wasn't the weather mild and nice and was the climb up the mountain very difficult? Would he like a warm cup of mead?

He was taken on a whirlwind tour of the castle, which was splendid. Up to the top of the tallest spire, a view from the ramparts, a glimpse of every room, chamber and den, it seemed.

Could I see the dungeons? Most certainly. Are they occupied? He would have to wait and see. Sinister words, preceding an equally sinister descent into the deepest and darkest portion of the castle. Sparsely placed torches barely lit the way, and innumerable times the boy almost fled back up the spiralling staircase, especially at the thought that perhaps the old man's plans were of a nefarious sort. He trod boldly on, however, one eye warily on his guide, and was relieved when no attempts were made to incarcerate him. Instead, his host proved most informative.

"To your right, at one time the cell of a sorcerer imprisoned for transforming chickens into gophers. A distressing habit, very unsettling economically.

"Look closely at the next, lad, and see the bloodstains of a great ruffian, murdered by his cell mate, a woman, incensed at his manner of ogling the siren in the cell beyond." On and on the narrative went, a tale for every cold and empty cell.

Then, because he had come this far, the boy said, "The wizard," and the old man turned an inquiring eye his way.

"The wizard," the boy repeated, half expecting that with a flourish and a self-deprecating laugh his guide would reveal himself as the famed necromancer and cast a modest spell or two.

"Eh? What?"

"I would like to meet the wizard who lives here, if I may," the boy said hopefully.

"Oh," the old man said. "Well." He shook his white-haired head. "No wizards here."

"But he lives here," the boy insisted.

"No, he doesn't," the old man said. "Used to, once upon a time."

"Where did he go?"

"Away. Where wizards go. Left with a gaggle of geese one day."

It was not beyond the realm of reason for the boy. He nodded politely and turned away.

The old man was an empathic soul who felt keenly the boy's disappointment. "A moment," he said, "wait a moment. There is magic about yet, I think, for the wizard could not take it all with him," and he led the boy back up through the convoluted castle corridors to a place they had not yet been.

They entered first a room of odd creatures. Cats and dogs as one, a creature with an extraordinarily long nose, horses with wings, multicoloured rabbits, and other magical animal fare. The boy murmured all the right things in all the right places, but he could not help but think that animals were animals, magical or not.

Next came a room of whistles and bells, of baffling machines that could perform every conceivable task, some that could potentially release mankind from its bondage of labour forever, others that could give it something to do then.

"Thank you," the boy said. "They are very nice. I believe my mother would have liked that one," and he pointed to a whirring contraption that diced carrots into a neat little orange pile. But the old man could tell that he was still disappointed.

In the spacious corridor he confronted the youngster. "Does the magic I have shown you fail to bedazzle? Does it not boggle your eyes, mystify your brain, make your nose runny? Do your knees not shake, your lips tremble, and your ears go all a quiver as you contemplate the magical prowess required to even imagine, let alone create, all that you have seen?"

The boy replied, "I have seen many wondrous things, I agree," and in truth he was impressed, at times it was all he could do to keep his ears from quivering and his nose from running. "It is just that I would have liked to have seen the wizard, is all," he said.

"Yes, the wizard," the elderly caretaker repeated. "A very great and popular wizard he was, it is understandable that you should so wish to see him. He has, however, flown with the geese, he shall not be back for a while, a century or so, I should imagine, so put it out of your mind. You shall not be able to see the wizard today. May I suggest some grapefruit juice in lieu?"

The kitchen had seven ovens and the pleasant scent of baking bread and basting turkeys was as permanent as the squared stone floor. Grapefruit juice was one of an abundant store of refreshments to choose from, so with his host's hearty recommendation, the boy bravely chose a green elixir instead, and they retired to the dining room.

It was there beneath an elaborately jewelled chandelier of enormous breadth, a gift from the gods, the old man claimed, that the boy humbly asked, "How did you come to be caretaker of this castle? Was your father a caretaker too? Or did the wizard make you, like he made the magical machines and animals, maybe out of a fly or a garden gnome?"

The caretaker replied, "I was neither born for the position nor created for it. Nay either did I covet it. I was chosen by the great wizard himself one day as I toiled in my father's field, and the wizard passed by and took note of my diligence and discipline and extraordinarily intelligent demeanour. Forthwith I was snatched away and a doppelgänger placed in my stead. I have been here since, happily so, I might add."

"I had thought you might be the wizard, hiding your true nature," the boy confessed.

"A common misconception," the caretaker reassured him. "It happens all the time. Perhaps it is my eyes, which are veritable pools of wisdom, and my kindly disposition, and my overall bearing of benevolence and tranquility. Why, I would have made a fine wizard looking the way I do. I look more like a wizard than the wizard himself, if the truth be known. However, I have never had an inclination to be one. Too much time with your nose in a book, studying spells. Hard on your eyes, hard on your nose." The old man shook his head. "Not for me."

Another round of green elixir and grapefruit juice. A chill invaded the room and prompted a fire in the hearth. Comfortable surroundings and pleasant company gave rise to prolonged conversation, though the caretaker spoke mostly, responding to the many inquiries of the boy.

"He calls it an elephant," he responded to one such question, concerning one of the magical animals they had seen. "Named for a distant relation, I'm told. The elongated nose concept arose from the wizard's fondness for noses, or perhaps more precisely, his fondness for the sense of smell. Smells are very important to the wizard. They alert your mind to many memories, you know, and the wizard is old and has many memories, many of which he cannot remember. He would like to recall more, and he believes that if he could smell better, he could remember better. It seems to have worked in the case of the elephant. However, it would be unseemly for a man to have a nose as long."

"Why did the wizard leave?" the boy wanted to know.

"I do not know for certain." The caretaker reflected on the question. "To see the world through the eyes of a goose, perhaps. It is a pastime he cherishes, seeing the world through different eyes, one day a goose, the next a dog. The world is a wondrous place, he says, but more than that, it is a trillion worlds, each unique and worth seeing. And each separate world may only be seen by looking through a fresh pair of eyes. So this time, I think, the wizard has chosen to live for a while in the world of a goose."

The boy smiled at this charming but unlikely hypothesis, considering that the wizard in question had to be a worldly, busy individual, with far better things to do than spend a hundred years as a goose.

A window revealed the sky outside to be of a beckoning hue, so with great reluctance but commendable discipline the boy stood and thanked his host for allowing him to stay for as long as he had. The tour had been magnificent, the magic unforgettable, and the refreshments most refreshing. The elderly caretaker in turn remarked that his guest was too gracious, and wouldn't he come again sometime?

They parted on the drawbridge. A shake of hands and a wave or two and then the heavy wooden portal clanked shut. Soon it was concealed behind a raised drawbridge. The boy stood gazing at the fairy tale castle for some time, prolonging the visit, which had been perfect in every way except for the absence of the wizard. He would visit again, if he could, and maybe by then the wizard would have returned. Surely he wouldn't really be gone for a hundred years.

Only when he had climbed all the way back down the mountain and caught the scent of the foliage there did the wizard remember. He smiled and sat and spent many hours recalling the visit to his home, through the eyes of a boy. How the familiar and mundane had been transformed! How it had appeared so fresh and wonderful! Then, he arose, touched his earlobe the requisite way, and borrowed new eyes for a walk in yet another world.

3

FIZZ

They came in the night, dressed in black, just as Archie was reaching into his fridge for a bottle of Fizz. They got to him before he got the Fizz, airborne dispensers drugging him well before the intruders even entered the house. They carried him out in a sedative-induced haze. Archie returned to his senses in an unfamiliar hover car, thoroughly annoyed. He hadn't got to drink even a single drop of Fizz. He sure had craved a sip.

"What do you want?" he asked the two men book-ending him in the hover's backseat. "Don't have much in the way of money. Think maybe you got the wrong guy."

One of Archie's abductors smiled,

revealed a set of gleaming white teeth. "It's not your fortune we want, Archie. Just a few bucks here and there."

The man's blue eyes sparkled beneath a head of beach boy blonde hair, his tan at odds with the snowflakes dappling the moonlight outside the hover. He looked like a walking advertisement for a product Archie had been hearing a lot about recently—something called The Vibe—some kind of genetic makeover promising eternal youth, or the next best thing. Archie couldn't afford The Vibe and wouldn't want it even if he could, but it seemed as if he couldn't turn around without hearing or reading about it.

The advertising industry had been getting way out of hand lately. The very air you breathed was thick with advertising. Why, you couldn't flush your toilet without fresh new ads popping up in your toilet bowl. Archie blamed deregulation for that, and for the greatest problem he faced in life, his current abduction notwithstanding: a dearth of his favourite soft drink, Fizz.

The makers of Fizz were people of integrity. They marketed their product with restraint, believing that Fizz stood on its own merits, that blaring its name from the rooftops was unnecessary. Their integrity had done them in. Shops no longer sold it, because no one was buying it, except for Archie and his wife. Seeing the writing on the wall, Archie had bought as much Fizz as he could afford. He figured he had enough for about eleven more weeks, properly rationed.

He had trouble rationing it properly.

"What do you want?" Archie asked Beach Boy.

Suddenly he had an irrational fear. They were after his Fizz. It wasn't inconceivable. He himself envisioned a time when a lack of the bubbly nectar might drive him round the bend, but then, a kidnapping seemed a mite extreme just to obtain a recently obsolete soft drink.

"Understand you like Fizz," Beach Boy said.

A chill ran up and down Archie's spine. "What?"

Beach Boy leaned forward. "Fizzzzz," he said in Archie's face. "What is it about that stuff anyway?"

"You can't have any," Archie said.

Beach Boy laughed. "We don't want your

stupid Fizz. Nobody wants Fizz. Haven't you noticed? They don't sell it anymore."

Archie waited.

Beach Boy leaned back. "So. What are ya gonna drink? What with Fizz off the shelves and all."

Archie had been giving that a lot of thought lately. He had discussed it ad nauseum with Rachel, until she told him that if he uttered another word on the matter she would divorce him. Archie continued to ponder the matter in private. There were only two soft drinks left on the market, and it had been a tough decision. But Archie had decided to go with the number two brand, Nutrilicious, because he had a thing for underdogs. If Nutrilicious ever became number one, maybe he'd switch.

But he wasn't about to tell Beach Boy that.

"Don't hurt Rachel," he said.

"Ah yes," Beach Boy said. "Married, three children, seven grandchildren. Pastor in a large church, popular preacher. Lots of friends. A man of not inconsiderable influence. Like to golf, dontcha Archie? Like to drink Fizz when you golf. Isn't that right?

Don't worry, Archie, your wife's not the problem. You, Archie, are the problem."

Archie felt the vehicle come to a halt. His abductors led him through a parking garage into a small nondescript room containing several chairs and a wooden table. Beach Boy took one of the chairs and indicated for Archie to take another. The other kidnappers remained standing. A short, squarish man entered, carrying three bottles and two glasses, which he placed on the table.

"Go ahead, Archie," Beach Boy said. "Pour yourself a drink."

"What is it? Poison?"

Beach Boy laughed. "Not as such. You're worth more to us alive, Archie."

"I'm not thirsty," Archie said.

Beach Boy pointed to one of the bottles. "This one's Fizz."

There was no turning down Fizz. Archie drank. Afterward, the short man produced a small handgun from an inside pocket and pointed it at Archie's left knee.

"Sample the rest," Beach Boy said.

"I thought you wanted me alive."

"A bullet in each kneecap and you'd be moaning but alive."

Archie sampled the rest. He recognized the bland taste of the other soft drink brands but couldn't tell which was which.

"Whattaya think?"

"Are you telling me you kidnapped me for a taste test?"

"Not just any taste test, Archie boy, the single most important taste test of your life. Now. Whattaya think?"

"Well, that Fizz sure was good. Could I have some more?"

"Sure you can, Archie. You can have as much as you like, later. But first, what did you think of the other two?"

Everyone in the room leaned forward to hear what Archie would say. "The first one was flat, insipid. Tasteless, really. Yet sugary, with a bitter aftertaste—"

"That much we know already. What about the second one?"

Archie made a face. "Even worse."

Beach Boy shook his head. "Archie, Archie, Archie. Wrong answer."

Archie tried not to look at the short man with the handgun.

"Drink the Fizz, then," Beach Boy said, surprising Archie. "If that's what you want."

Something about Beach Boy's tone made
Archie balk. He told himself he didn't really
want any Fizz. Ah, but who was he kidding,
he pretty much wanted Fizz all the time. He
took hold of the entire bottle and drank a big,
wet slug of the stuff. Afterward he burped,
and felt... nauseous.

Beach Boy held forth the bottle. "Have
some more, Archie, go ahead. Drink all you
like."

Weakly, Archie waved him away. "No,
thank you."

"Strap him in, boys." Beach Boy smiled.
"Expect we'll be here awhile."

Archie remembered nothing the
following morning, of course. He even
felt quite spry. His wife Rachel was the first to
notice something amiss.

"Archie! What are you doing with all that
Fizz?"

"Had my fill of it," he said. "Just can't
stomach the thought of drinking any more."

"Huh!" said Rachel. "Who'd a thunk?"

Archie shrugged. "Gonna chuck it and try

out that other brand, what's it called, Nutrilicious."

Rachel wasn't about to argue, not if it involved cleaning out the basement. Realizing there would never be a better time to mop down there she made a beeline for the laundry room where she plucked a jug of Glo & Shine from the shelf above the dryer. Glo & Shine was her number one choice for mopping floors these days. Not because it made the floors cleaner than other products (it didn't) but because of its one unassailable virtue: it was the only disinfectant she'd been able to use for the past year the smell of which didn't make her want to vomit.

4

OF PLATYPUSES AND THINGS

Dave's death came as a bit of a surprise to him. Not that he particularly cared whether he lived or died; having had somewhat of a bleak attitude toward life, he'd never become all that attached to it. The manner of his death surprised him—although he'd heard stories of people dying similarly, he had never given the stories much credence, and certainly had never expected to die that way himself.

It happened as he walked home with a friend after class—a class in which the professor had managed to discuss both platypuses and proofs for the existence of God.

"I don't believe in God," Dave had said, failing to notice the faint rumble of thunder that emanated suddenly from the clear blue sky. "What kind of a God would create a world like this one? Full of misery, war, and hunger. The planet's coming apart at the seams, if you ask me. There is no God. If there were, he'd do something." The thunder grew loud enough for Dave to notice it, and he held out a hand to see if it encountered any raindrops. It didn't. "Where is this God, anyway? I've never seen Him, Her, or It. It's never introduced Itself to me."

When Dave's friend opened her mouth to reply, another more strident roll of thunder pre-empted her.

"Another thing," Dave said. "What kind of a God" —and here he raised his voice, unaware that as he did so the thunder was rumbling fiercely and approaching a peak of its own— "would create an animal as ridiculous looking as a platypus?" Dave laughed loudly, and the thunder climaxed angrily.

A dark, roiling cloud appeared in the sky and produced an elegant little lightning bolt of a golden yellow hue that sped gracefully through the sky and effortlessly turned Dave into a smouldering pile of fine black ashes.

No, Dave certainly had not expected to die like that.

Now, thoroughly dead, he stood ankle deep in a lavender mist and watched bemused as a tall, thin man with glasses and a short, pudgy man without glasses appeared suddenly from out of nowhere and approached him.

"I say there," the shorter of the two greeted him. "How do you do?"

"Not well, I should think," the tall man commented dryly before Dave could respond. He pursed his lips in the manner of one in the know. "At least, he won't be doing very well very soon."

"You are no doubt correct," the short man agreed.

The twain regarded Dave mutely for a moment.

"Are you in trouble," the tall man said suddenly.

"Doesn't look good at all," commented the short.

"Glad I'm not in your shoes."

"Wouldn't trade places with you in a million years."

The tall man moved behind Dave, where he placed his hands firmly on Dave's shoulders and propelled him forward.

"Hey!" Dave protested, but found that he was powerless to do anything except go where the tall man wanted him to go.

A clipboard appeared in the short man's hands as he marched along beside them. "Dave Smith, number one one two, four six one, five seven two B." He flipped a page. "Apathy, pessimism, slander, tsk tsk!" He glanced up at Dave. "Really, Mr. Smith." Back to the page, he read, "Sins, negligible. That's good."

"Basically just an attitude problem," drawled the tall man from just behind Dave's right ear.

"Let's hope He sees it that way," grimaced Shorty. The clipboard disappeared and he moved to whisper confidentially in Dave's ear, "I think you just caught Him in a bad mood."

"Very bad mood," agreed Tall.

"If you're polite, maybe you'll get off easy."

They propelled him through a doorway that blipped into existence before them, and entered a large, sparsely decorated chamber. Torches lining the walls provided a modest illumination. The only feature of note was a bronze throne next to the wall opposite the door. A middle-aged man with a beard fully two and a half feet long occupied the throne. He possessed a great leonine head of snowy, unkempt hair, and pale green eyes that tracked Dave's movements with interest. Tall and Short escorted Dave to a spot just before the throne, and then moved to stand on either side of it, facing Dave.

The man with the beard leaned forward to study Dave. He regarded him closely for some time before speaking. "You," he said. "You upset me this afternoon."

Dave's knees almost buckled and he had to exert quite an effort of will to prevent from trembling. He had a sinking feeling in the pit of his stomach that the Being in the throne was God. And God was glaring at him.

"In fact," God said, "you really pissed me off." The glare intensified.

Dave's eyes widened. "Did you just say 'pissed off'?"

"You have a problem with that?"

"What kind of language is that for God?"

"I'm God. I say what I like when I like."

"Oh?" Before he could stop himself, Dave said, "And what gives you that right? Might? Might makes right?"

Tall and Short shook their heads frantically, mouthing, no, no!

Dave winced and braced himself for another bolt of lightning. But when none came, and Dave found himself capable of opening his eyes, he saw that God appeared more quizzical than angry. Dave took a deep breath and drew himself up a bit. Perhaps, he thought, God respected him for his chutzpah. He permitted himself a small smile.

"It astounds me," God said, "that I could have created a creature so remarkably dumb."

Dave exhaled sharply.

God snapped his fingers. Shorty produced his clipboard from the air and presented it to God, who perused the clipboard silently. Abruptly he handed it back to Shorty, who made it disappear.

"Apathy," God snapped.

Dave recoiled at the force of the word. "What?"

"You heard me. Apathy! Explain yourself."

"Apathy." Dully, Dave tried to engage his brain, give the word some meaning.

Apathy.

Apathy! To not care, passionless, without feeling.

"Insensibility to suffering," God added. "What was the point of your life, Smith?"

Dave's eyes lit up and it was his turn to glare. "What do you mean what was the point of my life? What are you asking me for? You tell me what the point of my life was, dammit!"

Dave's words echoed nicely off the far walls of the chamber.

The silence that followed, however, was less pleasant. Short and Tall trembled on their respective sides of the throne. God glowered threateningly.

Dave lost his nerve and decided a strategic retreat was in order. "I mean, tell me what the point of my life was, p-please?" He laughed weakly. The laugh sounded foolish. He regretted trying it.

God appeared less angry. "It's quite simple, really. Your life had no point."

Initially, Dave was stunned by this response. He'd always suspected that life had no point, and had in fact voiced this opinion often, but to hear it stated by God himself, and with such finality! That was a bit of a shock.

But because he'd figured as much all along, he quickly recovered. "So life really is pointless," he said.

God laughed. A raucous laugh, underscored by a low, ominous roll of thunder. Nice touch, Dave thought of the thunder. Subtle yet effective. Really gave one quite a psychological edge.

"Fool," spat God. "All life is not pointless."

"Wait, are you saying that only my life had no point?"

"Maybe it's my fault," God mused, tapping a slender finger against one arm of his throne. "Perhaps I made your brain too small. It's a wonder you can think at all with a brain like that."

Dave clenched his fists. "Now wait just a minute. As far as I could see, life had no point. I mean, we've been trying to come up with a point since day one, and all we've come up with is a thousand different religions. Which is the right one? The one you're born in? I don't think so. And heck! Up until a few minutes ago, I wasn't even sure you existed."

"As I remember it," God leaned forward menacingly, "you were quite sure that I didn't exist." His emerald eyes locked firmly on Dave's, as he motioned Tall and Short forward.

"What kind of God would create a world full of misery," announced Short.

Dave winced.

"War and hunger," added Tall.

"Whole planet's coming apart at the seams." Short.

"Where is this God?" Tall.

"Platypus," finished Short.

"I took particular offence to the remark about the platypus," God commented sourly.

"Sorry," Dave apologized, unable to think of anything else to say.

"I created the world, Smith, but I'm not responsible for what's done with it, okay? I created it for you, not for me. Don't blame me for the mess you're making of it. And I've always been rather fond of the platypus. Don't be making fun of it." God scratched his beard. "That takes care of slander and the platypus. Now, how 'bout pessimism? And we haven't covered this apathy thing enough yet. Eh, Smith? What's with this pessimistic attitude of yours?"

Dave shrugged, as if that explained everything. When it became apparent that it didn't, he said, "What can I say? Life didn't look too good to me."

"Why not?"

"Well, the world's a mess."

"Really? Why didn't you do something about it?"

"Me? Why should I be the one to have to do something?" God was beginning to sound just like his parents, for crying out loud. Dave decided the time had come to take a stand. "You can't tell me how to live my life," he said, just loud enough to be heard.

"I beg your pardon?"

"You heard me. You can't tell me how to live my life."

"I am God. Your Creator."

"So? Uncreate me. See if I care."

"No." God's shoulders drooped slightly. "I'm afraid I can't do that."

Dave suppressed a grin, confident that he had just bested God himself in a verbal joust.

An instant later he realised how absurd that notion was. Even calling it a stalemate would be stretching it. He took another gander at his reflection in the pond, and sighing a big platypus sigh, padded softly away toward a stand of juniper on the other side of the meadow.

5

THE PITCH

I found a seat on the GO Train, opened my laptop, and sighed. I needed to finish a spreadsheet detailing all the latest DaletPlus NetXchange issues before a conference call on the matter at nine. There was a crazy amount of work left to do. Unfortunately, before I could isolate myself from the rest of the passengers with an insulating layer of headphones and iTunes, damned if a CBC Radio producer didn't plunk himself down in the seat opposite me.

"Kelly!" the producer said. "Long time no see."

This did not bode well. It wasn't that the producer was a bad guy. It was just that he'd been dead for five years and was known to be a talker. I would get little work done this morning.

I forced a smiled. "Hey Runciman, good to see you. Coulda sworn you were dead."

Runciman had indeed been found dead late one night in an editing suite still clutching a script in his cold, dead hands. The cause of death had never been conclusively determined, but it was commonly believed that his recording engineer had strangled him to death in frustration for demanding one too many edits. Runciman had been a notoriously demanding producer.

"Dead as the proverbial doornail," Runciman confirmed.

"And you've come back to haunt me now because...?"

"I have returned to atone for my many sins."

"What sins?"

"Sitting on development committees rejecting perfectly good ideas, mostly. It is my intention to atone for these sins by helping you with your radio show pitch."

"What radio show pitch?"

"The one you're going to write to help you get back to your true love, radio production."

"Thanks, but I'm good. I like management."

"Because you make so much more money?"

"Uh—"

"Cause your benefits plan is so superior?"

"Um—"

"Cause you like ordering people around?"

"I do like that part," I admitted. "For instance, I order you to leave me alone."

The ghost of Runciman ignored me. "I have arranged for you to be visited by three spirits during your commute this morning. The Ghost of Radio Archives, the Ghost of Radio Ideas, and the Ghost of Radio Yet to Come."

"Three spirits? I don't have time for that —the commute is only so long and I have a lot of work to do!"

"They're all experienced radio folk, perfectly capable of talking to time." The train pulled into Ajax station. "Speaking of which, my time's up." Runciman stood to get off. "Don't mess this up, Mahoney!"

Resolving to seek therapy at the earliest

opportunity, I shook Runciman's hand and watched as he got off the train.

A small, elderly gentleman wearing a bowler cap got on and took Runciman's place. I recognized him right away. "Hey, you're Allan McFee, former host of the CBC Radio show Eclectic Circus!"

"I was that man once," McFee intoned in his best announcer's voice, still smooth and honeyed despite his death over a decade earlier. "Now I am the Ghost of Radio Archives."

I was impressed. "It's a great honour to meet you, Mr. McFee. You were a great wit in your time."

"Whereas you are a great nit wit in yours."

"Why do you say that?"

"Because you gave up your dream of creating your own radio show to join the dark side," McFee explained. "I despised managers when I was alive."

"I enjoy being a manager," I said. "But I regret not creating my own radio show."

"It's my job to help you get that dream back, son," McFee said. "Grab on tight to my hat."

I did as McFee instructed and off we flew,

miraculously squeezing through the closed Go Train doors into the archives of radio past. I found myself in the Canadian Broadcasting Centre in Radio Drama Studio 212, where I had spent nine productive years making radio plays. A large cast was assembled on the floor with Ann Jansen directing. A younger version of me sat in the control room operating the Neve Capricorn console.

"I remember this," I told McFee. "We were adapting Canadian author Jane Urquhart's novel *Away* for radio. It aired on *Sunday Showcase* and *Monday Night Playhouse*."

"Since *The Rosary* first aired out of Moncton's CNRA in nineteen twenty-five, radio plays of all shapes and sizes have aired regularly in this country," McFee intoned, "on CBC Radio series such as *Sunday Showcase, Monday Night Playhouse, Vanishing Point, The Mystery Project, Monday Playbill, Nightfall, CBC Wednesday Night* and more."

"Thanks for that almost completely indigestible bit of exposition," I said. "It is true that radio drama once thrived in this great country of ours."

McFee touched his hat and whisked us elsewhere. Three gentlemen stood on a stage before three Neumann U-47 microphones. Other gentlemen leaned over various sound effects apparatus, awaiting their cues. The whole lot of them were flanked by an orchestra. An audience was present to witness the shenanigans. I listened as the actors delivered a high-octane sketch at a breakneck pace about an ancient Greek messenger running an impossible distance to deliver a message only to discover when he arrives at his destination that he has forgotten the message. At the punch line, the audience erupted into laughter.

I was ecstatic. I whispered to the ghost of McFee, "It's Peter Sellers, Spike Milligan and Harry Secombe back in their *Goon Show* days —these guys influenced everybody from *Monty Python* to the *Beatles*."

"And now they shall influence you. Note their absurdist, rapid-fire dialogue, their ground-breaking sound effects, and the resulting realism. Observe how the three actors play almost all the parts themselves."

"Yes, if I were to make a radio show, this is exactly what I'd make," I said.

"Not exactly," McFee said. "You would

incorporate elements of it, but you were more ambitious than that in the past."

McFee touched his bowler hat yet again and transported us to a studio where a younger version of me was arguing amicably with a friend with whom he'd once made a radio show pilot. Although one of the pilots had aired to a fair bit of acclaim, the show had not been picked up by the network.

My friend was saying, "The network's not going for it because you want it to be both light and dark. You can't do that. It has to be one or the other. I challenge you to name one other show in the history of entertainment that's both funny and serious at the same time."

"*La Vie est Belle*," the younger version of me said, naming one of my favourite movies. "*M. A. S. H. Buffy the Vampire Slayer. Rome.*"

My friend was clearly not convinced, but the conversation reminded me of my earlier ambitions and I felt a pang of regret at not having pursued them more aggressively.

"Man was made for joy and woe," the spirit of McFee quoted. "And when this we rightly know, through the world we safely go."

"That's it exactly," I said. "That's what I was trying to tell him. Sting, right?"

"William Blake. Shortly after this conversation you gave up your dream of making your own radio show and fled into management's squalid embrace."

"Somebody's gotta run the place," I said defensively.

"I'm dead," McFee said. "I can have no more dreams. You're still alive. You have no excuse." McFee touched the tip of his bowler hat yet again.

I jerked awake on board the GO Train. Just a dream, I thought with mixed emotions: a little disappointed to discover that I was not actually supernaturally obligated to propose another radio show, but at the same time relieved that I would not have to risk failing at it a second time.

Someone tapped me on the shoulder. I spun to find a snowy haired gentleman with large glasses smiling at me from the adjacent seat. "A is for Aardvark," he said with enviable enunciation.

I gaped at the spectre of Lister Sinclair, former host of CBC Radio's *Ideas*. "Let me guess. The Ghost of Radio Ideas?"

"Fiction reveals truth that reality obscures," Sinclair said.

"Are you suggesting that if we only broadcast facts we're not conveying the whole truth to the Canadian public?" I asked, gamely trying to keep up with the polymath that was Lister Sinclair.

"*Ein blindes huhn findet auch mal ein korn,*" Sinclair observed.

I gave up trying to keep up with the brilliant polymath that was Lister Sinclair.

"I wrote a great deal of radio fiction in my time," Sinclair said. "I must say I find its current absence from our airwaves deplorable."

"It's not all gone," I said. "There's a bit of satire. Some sketch-based comedy. That's about it, though."

"What do you propose to do about it?" Sinclair asked.

"Me? What can I do about it? I don't do production anymore. I manage a broadcast maintenance department, for crying out loud. Even if I were still in production nobody would listen to me. They probably get dozens of proposals every day. Radio drama costs too much anyway, and more cutbacks are coming."

The train pulled up at Pickering. Lister Sinclair stood. "I tried management once. Didn't quite work out. Perhaps you have a stronger stomach for it than I did."

He got off, his manner leaving me with the distinct impression that he was disappointed by my outburst but not particularly surprised. I shrugged the Spirit's reaction off. I was under no obligation to propose any radio shows just because a couple of ghosts said I ought to.

The lights switched off abruptly. When they came back on I found that I was standing outside radio drama studio 212. Someone concealed within a black cowl stood alongside me, his or her face completely obscured by the garment. I tried unsuccessfully to peer into the hood, but it was impossible to tell who or what dwelled within.

The black-cowled figure that I presumed to be the Ghost of Radio Yet to Come raised a skeletal finger toward studio 212. Or at least, at what had once been studio 212, for both control room and studio lay torn asunder. A slightly older version of me clad in an ill-fitting suit stood in the ravaged control room instructing members of my staff which equipment to keep and which to throw out.

I regarded this future version of myself with horror. Never in a million years would I decide to destroy my beloved radio drama studio. But I knew that if my boss ordered my future self to shut down the studio because the Powers That Be had dictated that it must be so, I would have no choice but to carry out the repugnant order, lest I lose my job.

"Answer me one question, Spirit," I said. "Is this the shadow of the thing that *will* be, or is it the shadow of something that *may* be, only? Make that two questions. Why am I suddenly talking like a character in a Dicken's novel?"

Still the Ghost pointed his bony finger toward the studio.

"Let me get this straight," I said. "If someone doesn't start making more shows with dramatic elements real soon the Powers That Be will decide to shut down studio 212 because future utilization reports will show that it's under utilized? So I have no choice but to pitch a radio show that will use the studio so that they won't shut it down. Right?"

The Spirit remained infuriatingly mute.

"I'm not the manager I was," I said. "And I will not be the manager I must have been but for this intercourse. Why show me this, if I am past all hope! . . . I will honour radio drama in my heart, and pitch another project as soon as possible. Oh, tell me I may sponge away the destruction of radio drama within the CBC!"

I awoke writhing uncomfortably in my seat on the Go Train, disturbed not only by the vision of seeing myself preside over the destruction of drama studio 212, but also by having so shamelessly plagiarized Dickens in the previous paragraph. To my enormous relief no spirits sat next to me on the train.

Inspired, I abandoned the spreadsheet I'd been working on, completed my radio show pitch, and submitted it to the Program Development Department that very day.

Unfortunately, the Program Development Department rejected my pitch. Not only that, they shut down the entire radio drama department for good, calling upon my own maintenance department to dismantle Radio

Drama Studio 212. I myself turned off the studio lights for the very last time, though it pained me grievously to do so.

For it is sad, but the fact is you can't reliably glean the future from a mute spirit in a cowl, and even the most well-intentioned of ghosts cannot always successfully influence the affairs of men—they are, after all, ghosts. Their time is past.

And not all endings are happy.

6

THE SCAPEGOAT

The nothingness moved impatiently along in what has been called the Void by some, the Great Neutrality by others, and the Space Between by yet others. It was waiting for the arrival of its nemesis—not a pleasant prospect—and as a result it had become quite irritable. The norm for this unique creature was such an extreme level of irritability that an ordinary mortal would have been hard pressed to discern a difference, but as the creature's minions would no doubt detect when it returned to its lair, it was decidedly more irritated than usual.

Subtly yet perceptibly a change began to occur in the form of the nothingness. Initially the change consisted of no more than the sudden appearance of two or three electrons, followed by a neutron. After a brief respite, six more neutrons appeared along with four electrons and a proton, and this so enraged the creature that it accidentally produced within itself an entire atom.

The creature was enraged because, apart from the one atom it had accidentally created, its form of nothingness was being altered into another form by an external force. The only force in existence capable of doing this was its nemesis, and this meant that the nemesis was now somewhere nearby.

The altering of form occurred swiftly and resulted in the creation of something with humanoid features. With a certainty buried deep within a rising pit in what was fast becoming a stomach, the creature knew that the form it was beginning to attain was that of the Original. It did not resign itself to this fate as it had never and never in the future intended to resign itself to any fate. It fought with every fibre of its essence against the transformation, mustering every ounce of its will and energy. It applied every trick it had ever learned about shape changing, and every trick relating to the mastering of another's will, and when neither of these worked, it tried just as hard to apply the tricks learned of a multitude of other vaguely related disciplines. Although master of a much larger repertoire of tricks than in previous meetings with its nemesis, the creature discovered with despair that the outcome of this encounter would be the same as those of the past: the nemesis prevailed, and hovered before the creature, who now bore the Original Form.

"Lucifer," the nemesis said.

Sullenly, the creature Lucifer faced its nemesis, and with an effort of will so dextrous it could only have been made so with many millennium of practice, it increased its level of sullenness to equal that of its irritation and envy. But as potent as this sullenness became, it did nothing to mar the beauty Lucifer now possessed. No words of description employed by any of the peoples of the universe could even begin to convey to anyone the faintest impression of how beautiful Lucifer now was.

When Lucifer finally saw fit to respond to the nemesis, he said, "You call me Lucifer. I do not like the name, but I suppose there's nothing I can do about it. You will call me what you will. The question is what shall I call you?"

The nemesis did not reply.

"I shall not call you my God, or simply God, because you are neither of those things to me. I shall not call you my creator because even though that is what you are, I refuse to honour you as such."

"Why is it important for you to decide what to call me?" the nemesis asked.

Lucifer did not ask his nemesis why he asked a question when the nemesis was supposed to know everything. For one thing, he suspected that the nemesis did not know everything, and just pretended to, to feed the conceit that Lucifer felt the nemesis harboured somewhere not so deep inside himself.

Also, Lucifer had asked that question many times before and the response had always been most unsatisfactory: "Now and then it serves my purpose to ask questions," was a typically frustrating response. So this time Lucifer refrained from asking and said instead, "It is important for me to decide what to call you because I have decided that it is so."

The nemesis had expected this response, but this did not prevent him from chuckling at it. It is said by some that the nemesis cannot laugh, because, the reasoning goes, laughter is a response mechanism to being surprised in a particular fashion, and if the nemesis does indeed know everything, then he cannot be surprised, and therefore cannot laugh. This is not entirely true, however, because laughter can sometimes be used as a demonstrative device, and in this case the nemesis used it to demonstrate to Lucifer that he was, above all else, good-natured.

As always, Lucifer chose to believe that his nemesis was laughing derisively at him, but he refused to let this deter him from pursuing his subject. "Henceforth I will call you my nemesis, as that is what I have always considered you. It is both what you have chosen to be and all that I will ever honour you as."

"Fine," the nemesis said.

Lucifer was offended at what he perceived to be the great underlying condescension inherent in this remark, but he resolved not to show his nemesis how offended he was.

"Why did you summon me?" he asked politely.

There was a considerable pause before the nemesis responded, and even Lucifer was not so insensitive as to be totally unaware of the gravity of concern that now enveloped his nemesis. Fully a year and a half passed in some parts of the universe before the nemesis felt fit to reply.

"There has been a lot of suffering recently," he said finally.

Considering his usual preference for oblique statements and his definite passion for confusing images and roundabout illustrations this was an unusually direct thing for him to say. But this forthrightness failed to jar Lucifer in the least, and he conjured himself up a chair in which to sit while the nemesis spoke.

"There's a lot you don't know, Lucifer. If only we could set aside our differences and I could again instruct you. All of creation would benefit."

Lucifer had heard these words before and so ignored them. Something in the distance caught his eye and he strained forward in his chair to try to make it out. When he was unable to do so, he increased his visual ability to the point at which he could.

It proved to be something not concrete and real, but a visual thought, undoubtedly from his nemesis. Lucifer did not want to watch the thought, but he decided that he would, if only to hasten the meeting along. Time was passing, and although plentiful it remained a valuable commodity in that it could only be used once.

The thought moved closer and expanded to encircle Lucifer. Its flickering essence portrayed the actions of beings born far away from the Void. The colours of its images and scenes contrasted brilliantly with the utter absence of colour in the Void. Lucifer did not find it difficult to adjust his eyes.

The scenes the thought depicted were from a world with which Lucifer was familiar. The people of this world had once been favourites of his nemesis but had been left to function in isolation now for nearly two millennia.

The abandoned world seemed in a state of almost irreparable disrepair. Lucifer chuckled softly as indications of the forsaken world's plight unfurled about him. A people struggled in a confusion born of billions of minds un-unified. The bold, grim colours of war flickered bleakly on Lucifer's face. Horrendous battles raged about him. Countless atrocities, malice by the people against both themselves and their world—hatred, killing, gross manipulations and mishandling of nature, all of these and much, much more played before Lucifer, and he looked upon all of it with great interest, although careful to maintain outwardly an air of contempt for this creation of his nemesis.

Far greater than incidents of war and atrocity in number were the individual acts of petty malice perpetrated upon one another by the people of the world. Deception and disrespect commonly marred individual relationships, and were together eloquently indicative of the state of the world's decay. Lucifer marvelled at the ability and propensity of the people to perform at one time or another every dark action their active, unfettered minds could conceive, and he wished he could watch them in the future, wondering if there was not something even he could learn from continued observation of these remarkable people. The contemplation was more a form of compliment than serious speculation.

Lucifer was not surprised to hear his own name uttered countless times; all of creation knew of his fall from grace. Many of the injuries these people inflicted upon themselves they blamed him for, which irritated Lucifer—only once had he ever interacted with this race, and that had been a mistake.

Lucifer watched the people writhing painfully in the throes of their turbulent, potentially perpetual adolescence a moment longer. Then he caused himself to look through the thought image at his nemesis. He cleared his throat thoughtfully, carefully weighed his words, and said, "What is the point of all this?"

His nemesis ignored the question. "You have altered the shape I created for you."

While his nemesis had been engrossed in maintaining the thought image, Lucifer had taken the opportunity to change his shape somewhat. A revoltingly raw, skinless tail, in style reminiscent of the tail of a rat, albeit significantly larger, protruded from his hind section. His face, before a paragon of beauty, was now grotesquely distorted and would have produced in a mortal a reaction of utter shock and revulsion, at the very least. His torso, too, was twisted and misshapen, the epitome of ugliness. Indeed, his entire appearance seemed designed to demonstrate the extremes to which ugliness could be taken, if one really tried.

"Do you like it?" he asked.

The nemesis surveyed Lucifer's new appearance with an air of polite interest. "No, I can't say I do."

Lucifer chuckled—a low, guttural sound, a masterful display of derision toward his nemesis. Though it lasted a mere two and a half seconds, had it been directed toward a mortal the resulting destruction of ego might well have prompted a suicide.

The nemesis appeared unconcerned. "I would like your opinion of my images."

In his mind's eye, Lucifer rapidly reviewed all that his nemesis had shown him, including that which he had not paid attention to at the time, but which his senses had nonetheless picked up and stored away. "There was no point to it, Nemesis. You are wasting my time."

"It was not my intention to waste your time."

"What, then, was your intent?" Lucifer asked bitterly, though he knew very well the intent of his nemesis: to lay before him the evidence of his crimes against the nemesis' people. He knew that his nemesis desired strongly to punish him for those crimes, terribly and unjustly, proof indeed that his nemesis did not know everything. As if any punishment could ever be worse than the one he had received ages ago: banishment from the universe simply for daring to interfere with his nemesis' great plan.

The nemesis re-established his thought images off to the side and gazed at them wistfully. Now and then one appeared that caused him visible pain.

He turned to Lucifer and smiled sorrowfully. "You were my most beautiful creation."

Instantly, to Lucifer's great and unrestrained dismay, he reverted to his original form of unspeakable and incomprehensible beauty.

"I wished merely for you to be with me, to watch with me. As a father might wish to share something with a son, or a friend with a friend. But I am in a sad mood, and have shared with you the watching of sad things."

Lucifer said guardedly, "I am not responsible for any of those things."

To Lucifer's great surprise, for he is far from knowing everything and is as a result often surprised, his nemesis agreed. "No, you are not. In their haste to shun responsibility many of my people blame you, but I do not."

Lucifer closed his eyes. Then he opened them and said huffily, "So you summoned me here to make false overtures of friendship." He spat the word friendship. "I have watched a montage of the follies of the most incompetent and bumbling of your creations. Flawed creatures that in their unfathomable stupidity strive to cause one another great pain. I am pleased that you absolve me of responsibility for their actions. But share with me no longer the folly of their lives."

Following this scornful dismissal of his nemesis' attempt at reconciliation, Lucifer executed an impressive series of transfigurations that his nemesis made no effort to halt. After assuming the likenesses of several ugly beings responsible for the most ruthless of the atrocities of his nemesis' world, he became once again a vast sea of nothingness, and began moving slowly away.

The nemesis accepted this brazen display of disrespect wordlessly. He maintained an aloof air as Lucifer returned from whence he came to his den of unhappy minions and scurrilous plans. He was allowed to go because to stop him would change nothing. He was not responsible.

When he had gone, the nemesis turned back to his images and watched them silently for a long time.

He mourned the follies of his erring peoples.

And he mourned too the loss of a friend.

7

JOHN'S WORST ENEMY

Sleek and white, *Pegasus* sped off toward other stars, away from Dolmar 2 and its two tiny moons. Inside *Pegasus*, in the largest of the chambers adjoining the bridge, an alien artifact sat gleaming with silvery metal tubes.

The alien machine crackled and I saw John, reflected in a slender slab of the artifact, give a start.

"Aw damn, I've cut myself," he said, and he had, on a sharp edge. You had to be careful. There were many sharp edges.

John plucked a towel off what I had come to think of as the manifold of the alien artifact. Although to tell you the truth I had no idea what a manifold actually was; it was just a word I'd picked up from somewhere. He wiped some strange blue substance from his hands and inspected the cut on his index finger. He seemed concerned about getting the blue stuff in the cut.

"Did you cut yourself badly?" I asked.

The blood drained visibly from John's face at the sound of my voice. In contrast, a bright red blot welled up on his finger. Rudely, he ignored me. He placed the rag back down on the manifold and returned to work, and we worked together in silence for some time.

I could handle the silence for only so long. I decided to explore aloud my thoughts concerning the alien artifact. It would probably be wasted on John, who had the intellectual capacity of a gnu, but I didn't care. (I knew as much about gnus as I did about manifolds, but whatever they were, I had the impression they weren't particularly deep thinkers.) So I said, "I wonder what the people who built this machine were like?"

John stopped what he was doing.

"The artifact does bear a certain resemblance to human machinery," I continued. "Whoever they were, they obviously had opposable digits. Although judging by the size of the parts, their hands must have been at least twice the size of human hands."

John frowned. He held up an alien object that looked like a squished metal doughnut. He set it on top of a stubby pole that emerged from the compartment I thought of as the manifold and gave it a spin to get it going. It spun effortlessly down and around the pole until it reached the bottom.

"How do we know for sure this stuff is alien, Johnny?" John hated being called Johnny; I couldn't resist.

He gave a good look around the chamber before responding. I have no idea what he was looking for; we were alone aboard the ship.

"No human beings made this machine," he said.

"Oh?"

"Look what it's made out of. I don't even know what this stuff is. And I'm the first human being who's ever been out this far."

"You mean we're the first," I said.

I stared at John's reflection in the artifact. His pale blue eyes stared back. Wrinkles creased his forehead.

"It looks alien, too," he said. "Smells and feels alien. And I have no idea what the hell it is, couldn't even begin to guess what the. . ." he trailed off.

"Is something bothering you, John?" I asked.

He chewed on his lower lip. "You weren't here before."

I laughed. Sometimes John had the craziest notions. The thing about John, though, he never hesitated to say what was on his mind.

"That's it," he said. "You weren't here before."

He began to pace. It helped him to think, I knew.

"Something's wrong."

"Now, John—"

"Be quiet!" he snapped.

"For goodness sake, relax. Let's work on the artifact some more. It really is a beauty. It's gonna make us a fortune back home." The search for an alien object like this one had consumed much of John's life. Hard won it had been, but so worth the effort, if only he could manage to get it back home.

Mention of the treasure succeeded in

distracting John. I saw the pleasure in his eyes as he took in the machine's wonderful contours. He brushed a finger over a fluted edge. "You must have something to do with this machine."

As he fled from the room I had to hand it to John. Though not very bright, he was certainly a man of action. Had to be, or he wouldn't have survived out here for very long.

For instance, the time the meteoroid breached the hull and penetrated the oxygen reservoir. Another man might have panicked and simply sealed the compartment. The ship's main oxygen supply would have been destroyed within minutes. John, though, hit the pumps and flushed the reservoir's contents below decks. Only then did he seal the compartment. His quick action saved us, no question.

Of course, only an idiot would have allowed his ship to be struck by a meteoroid in the first place.

John raced to the medical bay and I with him. *Pegasus'* medical bay was quite reasonable for a ship of its size—John had ensured that this was so before leaving home, increasing an already severe debt load. All of his debts would be paid for several times over when he returned with the artifact.

"What's the matter, John? Aren't you feeling well? Maybe you should lie down for a while."

He ignored me.

"I should tell you, I find it very disturbing that you don't think I was here before. I hope you're not going crazy."

He drew a sharp breath at that.

We examined his reflection in a mirror. Sweat glistened on his brow. I thought he looked a bit pale. "You don't look well at all. Why don't you take an aspirin?"

"Shut up!" he said. "Or I'll—"

"What? What could you possibly do? Throw me out an airlock? Really, John."

He poured himself a glass of scotch and downed it. Afterward, I felt a thrill as he gripped the glass tightly—was he considering my suggestion about the airlock? But when he moved it was only to throw himself onto the diagnostic bench. He twisted the control panel until the unit hovered above his face. Punching several buttons, he set up a physical to include a blood work-up, a catscan, and an MRI. The diagnostic tube whirred forth and slid into place. It enveloped his entire body. He was supposed to lie still but I saw his fists clenching and unclenching.

As the program hummed about us, I asked, "Do you think you might have a cold or something, John?"

"You weren't here before," he said tightly. "I cut myself on the artifact, and then you were here."

When the program finished John lay motionless for several seconds. Then he pushed the tube back and swung to his feet. He punched a monitor on and we read the results of the tests together. They were fairly concise. Anything considered out of the ordinary was highlighted at the beginning. It looked like he didn't have a cold after all.

John mumbled some of the results aloud. "Damage to the corpus callosum. Hemispheric bicameralism. Cause unknown." He leaned heavily against the counter. I was afraid he might pass out. Indeed, I felt weak myself.

He managed to read further. The medical bay suggested that he be on guard for instances of catatonia and delusion, and that he be aware of the content and form of his thought patterns. It suggested dosages of chlorpromazine over regular intervals. Other than that, we read, nothing further could be done while onboard *Pegasus*.

John slumped in a nearby seat. I wondered if he was aware of his right foot tapping rapidly on the deck. "This voice is only in my head."

"That's ridiculous, John. I can assure you, I'm quite real."

He massaged his temples, hard. "You're just me, thinking to myself. The diagnosis was clear about that."

"Obviously the diagnostic system isn't functioning properly."

John stood and exited the chamber. I wondered if he even knew where he was going.

It required a special code to access the airlock. I knew it off by heart. Predictably for a man of John's limited intellect, the code was simply his wife and children's names coded numerically. John punched the number as I repeated it to him.

"Seven-two-two," I finished.

The first steel door shushed open. We smelled stale air.

John stepped forward. "I wonder if anti-psychotic medication would help?" he asked.

The door shut automatically behind us. With a dull thud and a series of sharp clicks, the mechanism locked securely into place.

"We don't carry chlorpromazine, John. Besides, those neural pathways have been destroyed."

I recited the code for the final panel. John stabbed at the buttons. The warning sounded and John looked surprised. We shared a magnificent view of our ship speeding off into space as the moisture on his tongue began to boil.

I managed to say just before his lungs burst, "Also, I think air pressure is really your biggest concern right now."

8

THE SCREW-UP

The technician listened uncomfortably as the Executive Producer talked about Rolf taking early retirement. Lots of people were doing it these days. Cutbacks. Golden handshakes. But Rolf... the department would go down the tubes without him. Rolf would go down the tubes without the department. Something about needing the package. Debts to pay off. Forced into it, really. Sad case. Wouldn't get his full pension now. The man had lived for his work.

The Department Head came in with the coffee. The technician took his black. The Department Head tried to give him his change, a whole nickel. The technician waved her off.

"So what happened the other day?" the Executive Producer asked.

The technician considered playing dumb but he hated people who did that. What day? Punish the Executive Producer for not being specific. Yes, the technician knew damn well what day. Something else the technician hated was making excuses, even if they were true. A point of pride. They hadn't been able to talk about it that day, but he had known it was coming.

He sighed. "Equipment."

"Equipment?" The Executive Producer knew that much already.

"Yeah. Bloody console."

Uncomfortable situation this, really. Fact was, as the sound technician it was his responsibility. He'd selected the equipment, tested it, set it up, tested it again, then tested it yet again. It wasn't his fault the audio console had decided to crap out just then. It was the console's fault. Blame the console. Except that it wasn't the console's fault. It was his fault, ultimately, because he was the technician, and it was his job to make sure things worked.

The Executive Producer was waiting to hear some more.

The technician stared back at him. Sure, he felt responsible. Wished he could have done more. Wished he'd chosen another console. Wished he'd been somewhere else that day. But he had been around long enough to know that these things happened, it was just plain bad luck, you got past it, moved on, forgot about it. The Executive Producer knew that.

"Did you test it?"

Holy cow, there was a question. Had he tested it? Of course he had tested it! Two, three times. The technician frowned. How to respond to this remarkably stupid question? This insulting question.

He said, "Yes." No need to add, "Of course".

"And it worked."

The technician wanted to say, "Well, no, it hadn't. But I used it anyway." But he was on shaky ground to begin with and sarcasm wouldn't help, even if deserved.

So he said, "Yes, it worked. Every time. All

three times I tested it, yes." That ought to drive the point home. The Executive Producer laughed. Because he wasn't exactly sure why the Executive Producer was laughing, the technician just sat there.

"Wow," the Executive Producer said. He shook his head. "What a screw-up, eh?"

The technician shrugged. "Well."

"They had to fill back at the station. Had to play fill music for the whole show." The Executive Producer laughed again. "Cause we sure as hell weren't there."

The technician refused to laugh. It wasn't funny, not to him, not yet. It was embarrassing, as embarrassing as hell. The whole live audience had been waiting, waiting for the show to begin. All the lines back to the station had been tested. He had done hundreds of these remotes before, they had become routine, but still there was always that moment of tension just before you went live. Would it work? Everything you had set up, would it get the signal back to the station and then out onto the air and make everybody happy? The producer? The host? Especially the host?

Then the moment was past and the host

was talking, the theme was playing and you were live, you were on, the producer was smiling, the host was smiling, the audience was smiling, you were smiling, everybody was as happy as pigs in poo.

Not this time. The moment was upon them and nothing worked. Nothing. Everything was dead. The host's mouth was moving and nothing was coming out. The Executive Producer was shouting, the host was freaking out. The audience was murmuring, wondering. In that instant, the technician checked a thousand things. The CD player didn't work, neither did the tape machine, the microphones, the wireless, nothing. It all pointed to the damned console.

"What is it? What's wrong?" the producer shouted.

"It's the console," the technician told him.

"What can we do?"

"Nothing. I didn't bring another one." And the station was too far away to go and get one. The technician never liked to beat around the bush, and he didn't see the point in doing so now. He hadn't brought a spare, and there was nothing they could do about it. All they could do was tell everyone involved that the show was over before it even began. Tear down and go home.

A bad day.

Now they were in the Executive Producer's office, going over it all again. The Executive Producer had stopped laughing. The Department Head was still there, and had yet to say anything. Nice of her to have brought the coffee, though. The technician began to get annoyed. Where was this leading? It was time to stop beating around the bush.

He said, "Well, it was my fault, I apologized to everyone already. I should have brought a spare console. I don't know why I didn't."

Were they going to fire him? Or just make him feel bad? He waited. He'd said his piece, laid his head on the chopping block. The ball was in their court.

Then it struck him. Rolf. Early retirement. That's why the Executive Producer had started this meeting by mentioning Rolf! They weren't going to fire him, they were going to make him accept some stupid package! Get rid of him that way. It all made sense. He wanted to lean across the desk and choke the Executive Producer, choke the life right out of him. It wasn't his fault, it could have happened to anyone!

The Executive Producer was being cruel. He had a goofy grin on his face. The Department Head was smiling too. How could they be so heartless? "Yes sir, quite a screw up. Biggest one this corporation has seen in a while."

"So you're going to force me out."

The Executive Producer looked puzzled. "What?"

"You're getting rid of me, right? No more embarrassing mistakes," the technician said bitterly. "You're going to force me to accept a package."

"Hell no."

"What then?" What else was there?

The Executive Producer leaned forward. "You have a gift for screwing things up. That means you have a bright future ahead of you in public broadcasting."

The Department Head extended her hand. "Congratulations," she said. "We're making you a manager."

9

AUTHOR'S NOTES

Moonstone is my tribute to the work of Fritz Leiber. I've always loved the swords and sorcery genre, especially Leiber's Fafhrd and the Gray Mouser series. But that's not entirely what inspired Moonstone. One day, back around the turn of the century, I read an obscure swords-and-sorcery tale in an obscure magazine no longer in publication—I can't remember the name of either. I enjoyed the story but thought, "I can do better." I don't know that I did, but I certainly tried. Moonstone took me about a year to get right.

I wrote The Wizard's Castle in a few short hours one summer day. I wrote it in longhand, like every story I wrote before I got my first computer in the early nineties. It was one of those rare occasions when the words just flowed, although it did require a bit of buffing up before I sold it to Horizons SF. In 2005, Barbara Worthy produced a version of the story in which an actor performed the text while playing the piano. If you flew Air Canada around then you could have heard this version on Air Canada's in-flight channel KidzAir.

Fizz took a few drafts to get right. Graeme Cameron included it in the third issue of Polar Borealis, a magazine of Canadian SF.

Of Platypuses and Things is another rare instance of the story virtually writing itself. This was before I acquired the unfortunate habit of editing my writing as I went along, a terrible habit that I'm only now overcoming. Of Platypuses and Things found a home in an Australian magazine called Planet Relish.

The Pitch is the only story in this collection never to have been published before. It was never meant to be a short story at all. It was originally written as just what its title suggests: a pitch for a show on CBC Radio. I've tweaked it slightly for this anthology. Sadly, The Pitch did not result in an actual radio show. And the powers that be did eventually shut down radio drama studio 212, along with the entire CBC Radio drama department.

The Scapegoat is the oldest story in this collection, completed on September 26th, 1987, when I was twenty-two years old. The Canadian magazine Challenging Destiny bought it for its April, 2000 issue. It's the first short story I ever sold.

John's Worst Enemy was inspired by a psychological hypothesis called bicameralism that argues that at one time the two hemispheres of the brain were essentially distinct from one another, creating the impression of two entities residing within a single body. Some in the scientific community speculate that this may have been a fact of life for pre-historic humans, before their brains evolved into the ones we currently possess, though vestiges of this phenomenon may remain in some of us today.

I belonged to a union in a tumultuous relationship with management when I wrote The Screw-Up, back in the late nineties. I was, in fact, on strike in 1999 when Our Times: Canada's Independent Labour

Magazine published the story. Less than a decade later I became a manager myself (not because I screwed up a remote, though), so really, I'm just making fun of my future self. These days I have a much more charitable attitude toward management.

ABOUT THE AUTHOR

Joe Mahoney worked full-time for the Canadian Broadcasting Corporation for thirty-five years. There, he spent a decade making radio plays, working with some of the finest actors, directors, and writers in Canada. He joined the management team after that and helped run the place.

His debut novel, A Time and a Place, was published in 2017 by Five Rivers Press. His memoir, a behind-the-scenes glimpse of working at CBC Radio, Adventures in the Radio Trade, was published in 2023 by Donovan Street Press. He's also worked as a story editor on multiple radio, television and film projects.

Joe is a member of SF Canada, Canada's National Association of Speculative Fiction Professionals, and SFWA, the Science Fiction & Fantasy Writers Association.

He lives in Riverview, New Brunswick with his wife Lynda, their Sheltie Wendy, and their Siberian Forest Cat Lily.

ALSO BY JOE MAHONEY

Fiction:

A Time and a Place

Nonfiction:

Adventures in the Radio Trade

As editor:

The Deer Yard and Other Stories (by Tom
Mahoney)